Ricky Rides The Pine

PRAISE FOR *STORYSHARES*

"One of the brightest innovators and game-changers in the education industry."
– Forbes

"Your success in applying research-validated practices to promote literacy serves as a valuable model for other organizations seeking to create evidence-based literacy programs."

- Library of Congress

"We need powerful social and educational innovation, and Storyshares is breaking new ground. The organization addresses critical problems facing our students and teachers. I am excited about the strategies it brings to the collective work of making sure every student has an equal chance in life."
– Teach For America

"Around the world, this is one of the up-and-coming trailblazers changing the landscape of literacy and education."
- International Literacy Association

"It's the perfect idea. There's really nothing like this. I mean wow, this will be a wonderful experience for young people."   - Andrea Davis Pinkney, Executive Director, Scholastic

"Reading for meaning opens opportunities for a lifetime of learning. Providing emerging readers with engaging texts that are designed to offer both challenges and support for each individual will improve their lives for years to come. Storyshares is a wonderful start."
- David Rose, Co-founder of CAST & UDL

Ricky Rides The Pine

Kyle A. Johnson

STORYSHARES

Story Share, Inc.
New York. Boston. Philadelphia

Published in the United States by Story Share, Inc.

Storyshares
Story Share, Inc.
24 N. Bryn Mawr Avenue #340
Bryn Mawr, PA 19010-3304
www.storyshares.org

Inspiring reading with a new kind of book.

Interest Level: High School
Grade Level Equivalent: 3.8

9781642611762

Book design by Storyshares

Printed in the United States of America

Storyshares Presents

1

Ricky loved football as much as he hated homework.

"Who cares about homework, Grandma? I'm not gonna need school when I become a pro football player," Ricky said. He tossed his English notebook against his bedroom wall.

"I care, Ricky," Grandma Braun said, blowing on her glasses to clean them. "Someday football might not be an option anymore. Something might happen so you can't play. You need your education. Pick up your notebook. That's no way to act."

Ricky retrieved the notebook he had thrown. "Fine. I'll do my homework, but I gotta go to my game soon," he said. He sat at his desk to try to write a book report about a book he did not read.

He worked on it until it was time to go.

As Grandma Braun drove to the field, she gazed at Ricky for a long time. It seemed like she did not blink. Ricky tried to ignore her by looking out the passenger-side window.

Her brown eyes remained on Ricky. "I only want the best for you, honey."

To her, it seemed like Ricky had grown up so fast. One moment he was a baby in her arms, and the next moment he was a junior in high school. Ricky's grandparents had raised him since the day he was born. Ricky's dad went to prison a month before he was born. They did not have contact with each other. His mother was invisible. She gave birth to Ricky and never wanted to see him again. When he was ten, his granddad died of a heart attack. Since then, Ricky and his grandma lived by themselves in an apartment in Wellsport.

"I'm not saying you can't be a superstar football player. You are fantastic. You need to remember that your education is also important. I don't want you to forget that," Grandma Braun said.

When they got to the field, Ricky slammed his door. His cleats clicked against the gravel as he walked to the trunk of the car. He grabbed his equipment—a helmet and shoulder pads—from the trunk. The trunk hatch made a loud thud as he closed it.

Ricky frowned. "See ya later," he said.

"By the way you are looking at me, you appear to be upset," Grandma Braun said. "That look better be erased from your face after the game."

2

When he got to the field, Ricky's frown disappeared. Football did that for Ricky. It was the only thing that did. He was excited to learn everything about the sport. In math class, it was a lot more fun to daydream about football games than to think about multiplication problems.

Ricky liked football because he was really good. He was the most talented running back on the team. He had been playing since he was eight, and he was used to being the best.

Ricky was the fastest and strongest player on his team. Last season, he used bursts of speed to run past the defenders. He also used his strength to run over them. He scored eighteen touchdowns in only six games. He also had five fumbles, but he preferred not to talk about those.

Last season, his team had three wins and three losses. They missed making the playoffs by one game. Ricky's fumble in the last game cost his team the win. He was careful not to think about that, though. Ricky chose to remember the four touchdowns he'd had.

This was going to be Ricky's best year yet. He knew highly respected colleges were going to watch him. Ricky trained all spring and summer to get ready for football season. He devoted all of his time and energy to football. He didn't do much else.

Ricky's main goal for the upcoming season was to impress the scouts. He wanted to score at least twenty touchdowns. It did not matter to him if his team, the Wellsport Warriors, won or lost.

At practice, leading up to the first game, Ricky was unstoppable.

He looked smooth running the ball. Sometimes, he jogged, then suddenly changed speeds to run by the defense. On other plays, he made defenders miss and kept his balance to stay in bounds. Every time he showed his talent, his teammates shouted, "Nice run! Good job! You're the man!"

Sometimes Ricky's teammates put up their hands for high-fives, but he mostly just ignored them.

One time, he ran past them to the bench for a drink of water. His long touchdown run made him thirsty. Ricky sat on the right end of the bench, away from his peers. The rest of his team huddled near each other on the opposite end.

Coach Daniels, who had a whistle around his neck and wore a visor to shield the sun from his eyes, walked over to Ricky. "You should be very proud of your achievements. You did things today I've never seen anyone else do." Ricky nodded as if he were listening to his coach. He was not.

It was going to take something drastic to happen to change Ricky's attitude.

3

"Welcome to Dundee Field," the announcer's voice echoed. "Today's game is the Yorkdale Dragons versus the Wellsport Warriors." The spectators, family and friends of both teams, were ready to watch the game.

The Dragons won the coin toss and decided to receive the ball. Wellsport's kicker, Eric Gonzalez, booted the ball to Yorkdale's kick returner. Yorkdale made a solid wall to block the Warriors. The returner made two players miss, then he galloped like a horse in the open field. He was not touched by the time he reached the endzone. He easily scored a touchdown. The Dragons made the extra point to take a 7-0 lead.

"Just wait until I get the ball," Ricky said, under his breath. He did not care that the Dragons were winning. He did not care if the Warriors won or lost. As long as he scored a few touchdowns, he was happy.

When Wellsport had the ball, they marched straight down the field. The team relied on Ricky. They gave him the ball three times in a row before he scored a touchdown.

He was thrilled with himself. He danced alone in the end zone. "Ha! Yeah! Look at me. I'm gonna be famous someday. You're gonna know the name Ricky Braun," he said, pointing at himself.

The referee, a man with gray hair, blew his whistle and threw a bright-yellow penalty flag. Ricky had broken the rules by boasting about himself. The penalty did not prevent Ricky's selfishness. He scored two more times in the first half. He still boasted and bragged each time he scored.

At halftime, Coach Daniels and Ricky's teammates were upset that he kept breaking the rules.

Dashawn Berry, Wellsport's quarterback, pulled Ricky aside. "Man, you have to stop doing that. You are so valuable to our team. You have scored all of our points, but you are hurting our defense," he said.

Dashawn was right. The Warriors were ahead 21-7 because of Ricky's talent.

However, each penalty gave the Dragons a better chance to score.

Coach Daniels called Ricky over. He said, "Remember you are part of a team. Be smart out there, buddy." Wellsport got the ball to start the second half.

The coaches began calling plays for other players. Dashawn threw the ball to Marcus Swan on first down for a sixteen-yard gain.

Next, Jerome Davis, the full back, got the ball three times in a row. The Dragons prevented him from getting a first down. The Warriors had to punt.

Ricky did not understand. He was used to getting the ball on almost every play. "Coach, why didn't you give me the ball? I can score every time I have my hands on it," he said.

"I know you can, Ricky. But there are other players on the team. They also deserve a chance to play. They have put their time and sweat into practicing, too. They have worked really hard."

His peers heard the entire conversation. They were getting fed up with Ricky's attitude.

"I don't need those fools," he said. He pointed his finger at his team. "I can beat the Dragons with no help. I can beat them alone."

His whole team stayed silent. They shook their heads in disagreement. They knew he was wrong.

The next time the Warriors got the ball, the coach called a play for Ricky. He took a pitch from Dashawn and broke one tackle. A player for Yorkdale finally brought Ricky to the ground.

A snapping sound, like a tree branch in a windstorm, echoed through the stadium.

No one said a word. Everyone was silent.

Everyone except for Ricky.

4

"My leg! I broke my leg," Ricky howled. He rolled around on the field.

His teammates were stunned. They did not know what to do. The coaches ran to Ricky. His brown cheeks were soaked with tears from the intense pain. They examined his injured leg. Everyone heard the snapping noise. They knew he was hurt badly.

Grandma Braun ran to the field from the quiet, surprised crowd. "Oh my goodness. How bad is it?" she asked Coach Daniels.

"It's terrible," he said. "He broke his leg. He's suffering right now. He needs to go to the hospital."

Ricky's coaches and teammates helped him to his feet. He could not walk, so the coaches carried him to Grandma Braun's car. As they carried him, they were careful not to bump his leg. He was in a lot of pain.

They carefully placed Ricky in the back seat, so he could stretch out his leg. It hurt too much to touch or to bend.

Grandma drove swiftly to the hospital. She sped the whole way because of Ricky's serious injury.

At the hospital, they met Doctor Jones. She took Ricky to get an x-ray.

The doctor looked at the film. "Ricky, you have a broken tibia," she said. "That is another name for your shin. The front part of your lower leg."

"It is all my team's fault. They didn't block for me. I have a broken shin because of them," Ricky said.

Grandma disagreed with Ricky. She asked the doctor to leave for a few minutes. When they were alone, Grandma said, "You are wrong, Ricky. You only have yourself to blame."

She explained to Ricky that it was his fault he got hurt. His bad attitude made the other Warriors angry. They were offended that Ricky said he could beat the Dragons by himself. They did not block as well as they normally did.

Doctor Jones returned to the room. She came back to explain what happened to Ricky's leg. "It seems like when you got tackled, there was too much pressure on your leg. That is how your leg became fractured."

The doctor said Ricky's leg was going to be in a cast for at least two months.

Ricky didn't understand. "But when will I be able to play football again?" he asked.

"You will not be able to play again this season," Doctor Jones said. "I am very sorry, Ricky."

Ricky could not believe what he was hearing. "But, I need to play," he said.

"You will be in a cast and on crutches. There is no way you can play this season," Doctor Jones said.

All Ricky cared about was football. His heart sunk.

5

Ricky and Grandma Braun had an important talk at dinner the next evening.

"I'm not going to practice anymore," Ricky said, scooping mashed potatoes in his mouth.

Grandma sliced the meatloaf she made. She put a chunk on Ricky's plate. "Why not?" she said.

"It doesn't make sense for me to go. It's not like I can play," he said.

He tapped his hard cast and pointed at the crutches leaning against the wall. He looked down at his plate. He pushed his peas with his fork to avoid eye contact with Grandma Braun.

"Well, I am sorry you feel that way," she said. She took a deep breath. "Are you sure you don't want to watch your team practice tomorrow?"

Ricky thought for a moment. He surveyed her kind face. The wrinkles on her mocha-colored skin were well earned. So were the swirls of white and gray on her head. Her hair looked like fresh snow piled on stones.

"My leg is too sore," he said. It was true. His leg ached. It was the worst injury Ricky ever had. Even so, he could have watched his team practice. He did not want to watch his team have fun without him. He was being selfish again.

Grandma Braun let out a sigh. "You need to go watch your teammates," she said.

Ricky crossed his arms. "Ugh. Why? It's not fair."

Grandma looked across the round dining room table to see Ricky's body language. For a moment, she wondered where she went wrong raising him. She tried to figure out when he started to act that way. Grandma decided that she did not fail. Ricky was simply acting like a teenager.

"You are right, honey. It isn't fair. It isn't fair to anyone. Not your team or coach. Not to me. Not even to yourself," she said.

"But Grandma," Ricky started to say.

"No buts. I didn't raise you to be an uncaring brat. You are better than this. You need to cut out this 'me-first' mentality you have," she said.

Ricky huffed. He turned his head toward the television. He glared at Grandma Braun out of the corner of his eye. Grandma picked up her plate from the table. She walked toward the kitchen, then paused. "You can ignore me all you want. Someday I won't be around anymore. You need to know that your actions are a reflection of the people around you. When people see you acting selfishly, they think it's my fault. When people see you dancing like a fool after a touchdown, they think it's my fault or the coach's fault. We all know who really is to blame."

Ricky knew it was his fault, but he was too proud to admit it.

6

Much to his dismay, Ricky went to practice the whole week. He told Grandma Braun he would go. He never told her he would enjoy it.

He sulked on the sideline for the entire practice. His teammates did tackling drills and practiced plays. He sat on the bench deciding what animals the clouds looked like. Sometimes he would see how often he could catch his crutches before they hit the ground. His record was forty-one.

Ricky thought distracting himself was better than watching his team play without him. He did not wish to see his replacement, Keith Harris, take his spot.

If Ricky was paying attention, he would have noticed Keith had improved from last season. Through hard work and listening to his coaches, Keith had become a fine replacement for Ricky.

The Warriors entered their second game without their star player. Ricky expected that the Newcastle Knights would dominate the Warriors. He thought that the Warriors would not score any points without him.

As it turned out, Wellsport played better without Ricky. Without Ricky's careless fumbles or selfish penalties, the Warriors dominated Newcastle. They played as a team and won 35-0.

So, as a team, the Warriors celebrated on the field.

"Yeah! We did it!" Dashawn said. "Can you believe how well we did, man?"

Ricky politely smiled and gently slapped Dashawn's helmet. "Yeah, it's great," he said. Ricky thought to himself, *It's a fluke. There's no way they can keep playing this well without me.*

Dashawn grinned back at Ricky. "Wasn't Keith great? Those two TD's? The offensive line was awesome today. They blocked really well for him."

Ricky bit his tongue. "Yeah, they were great," he said. He really thought: *I'm a better running back. The offensive line is the reason why my leg was broken.*

His team had won, but Ricky felt like he had lost.

7

At school on Monday, Ricky felt even more like a loser. His lack of interest in school caught up with him.

As usual, Ricky did not pay attention to anything his history teacher said. Ricky focused more on the ticking black hands of the clock. To Ricky, it seemed like he had been in first period for three hours.

Ricky tapped his broken pencil tip against his desk waiting for the bell to ring. Finally, the harsh metallic clang signaled the end of class. The bell rattled awake two students in the back of the room. Other students tried to leave the room before Mr. Trout remembered to assign homework. Mr. Trout walked past a student with her hand raised. He called to Ricky. "Wait. I need to speak to you, please," he said. Ricky secretly kicked himself for not leaving fast enough. *Stupid crutches,* he thought.

"Yes, Mr. Trout?"

"What do you think your grade is right now?" Mr. Trout rested his index finger on his chin waiting for Ricky's answer.

"Um. I don't know. Why?" Ricky had been in the same position many times in previous school years. He expected Mr. Trout to yell at him.

"You are failing," he said. He walked a few steps toward Ricky. Ricky knew the yelling was going to start. Mr. Trout walked over to a wooden desk, which was attached to a blue chair. The chair's metal legs squeaked against the tile floor as he moved it closer to Ricky. "How can I help you?"

Ricky was confused. "What do you mean?" he said.

He looked Ricky in the eyes. "I know you can be a better student. How can we get you to where you want to be?" he said.

Ricky broke eye contact with Mr. Trout. "I'm where I want to be," he said.

Mr. Trout shook his head. "No way, Ricky. I do not believe that for a second. I have seen the competitor in you on the football field. I know you are a fighter."

Ricky disagreed with his teacher. "I like playing football. I don't like school. There's a big difference," he said.

Mr. Trout nodded. "I understand why you think that, but I am talking about effort. I am talking about how hard you try at something."

Ricky chuckled. "Why would I want to try at school? It's boring."

"We are only three weeks into school. This is a clean slate. A new chance for you to be successful at school. Look, you are in a cast. You are done playing football this year. Now, you can bring that same effort to school every day," Mr. Trout said.

Ricky sighed and hung his head. "I'm too dumb, Mr. Trout. I can't do this stuff."

"I promise that you can. I am here to help you do it. If you want to play football at a good college, you need to get your grades up," he said.

Ricky stared blankly at Mr. Trout. "I do? I thought I could get a football scholarship," he said.

"Football talent is part of it. You also have to have a certain grade point average to get accepted."

Ricky did not fully believe Mr. Trout. He was skeptical.

"Let's do this: get all of your missing work today. Then, we will meet here after school. We will work on getting you caught up."

"Really? You want to help me?" he said, raising his right eyebrow.

"I am positive. I want to help all of my students succeed. Ricky, I know you are smart enough to do this. We just need to get you to believe in yourself."

Ricky was an interesting young man. On the football field he thought he was the best. In the classroom, he thought he was the worst.

8

That week, Ricky's life was full of choices. They were choices that ended up defining his character. For one, Ricky decided to accept Mr. Trout's help. After school, Ricky brought his homework to Mr. Trout's classroom. Mr. Trout graded papers as Ricky did his homework. If Ricky had a question, Mr. Trout would help him figure out the answer. It was important to Mr. Trout that Ricky thought of the answer himself.

By the end of the week, Ricky had caught up on all of his missing assignments.

A new problem surfaced at school that week. Other kids at school teased Ricky about the football team winning without him.

A girl with braces named Tanya, who used to like Ricky, laughed at him. "They didn't need you," she said.

John, a boy who quit the basketball team last year, said, "You're just a benchwarmer. You're riding the pine. You're a nobody."

Ricky was not used to being bullied. He was used to being an untouchable superstar. He was used to people building him up, not tearing him down. The words of Tanya and John had the sting of a thousand hornets. Their words were harsh, but Ricky wondered if they were true.

For most of Ricky's life, he did not feel accepted. He thought his mother did not want him. He thought his father chose a life of crime over him. The truth was, he loved football because it made people more accepting of him. He was so selfish on the field because he was clinging desperately to the one place where he felt like he belonged.

In one snap of the leg, all of the acceptance vanished. What was he to do?

He thought about the possibilities all day. Ricky made up his mind. After school, he swung his way through the locker room and to Coach Daniels' office. "We need to talk," Ricky said.

Coach Daniels sat at an oak desk writing on a clipboard. "Sure. Take a seat." The coach gestured toward an open chair across from the desk. "What's up, Ricky?"

Ricky rested his crutches against the brick wall. He hobbled over to the chair Coach Daniels offered him and sat.

Ricky looked down at the tan, square floor tiles. He folded his arms tightly and slouched in the chair. "I'm tired of this junk," he said, curling his upper lip.

"Ricky, what do you mean?" Coach Daniels said.

Ricky mustered the courage to tell his coach what he thought. "I quit. You don't need me. Nobody needs me. You win without me, anyway. Kids make fun of me now for not playing. I don't need this," he said.

The coach's face turned red, then he snapped the clipboard in half. "In my twelve years of coaching, I haven't seen a player as talented or as selfish as you, Ricky Braun." Tears welled up in the corner of the coach's eyes. Ricky had never seen his coach cry before. "You don't get it, do you? Your teammates have always been there for you. Now, you want to turn your back on them. Unbelievable."

Ricky was stunned into silence. Coach Daniels continued. "Your teammates need you. If you want to give up on them, you can. It is your choice." Coach Daniels stood and paced behind his desk. "Before you make your decision, let me explain that you can't go through life quitting when times get hard. You can't always quit when you aren't the star."

The truth hurt Ricky. He stood, then walked out of the office without saying a word.

It appeared Ricky had made his choice.

9

Coach Daniels was disappointed that Ricky chose his pride over the good of the team. He shook his head in disbelief as he turned off his office lights. He had a practice to run whether Ricky was there or not.

Coach Daniels entered the locker room. The room was dark, empty, and quiet. Normally, the room bustled with players putting on their equipment. He could usually hear the slamming of lockers and the loud conversations of students.

"Hello? Where the heck is everybody?" he asked himself.

Coach Daniels walked through the vacant locker room and opened the heavy metal door that led to the field.

He poked his head out of the door and saw the team and his coaching staff already on the practice field. Determined to figure out what was going on, the coach jogged to the field.

When he got there, he noticed his players were huddled around someone. Some of the team kneeled on the grass, while others stood. It was quiet except for one voice.

It was Ricky's voice that commanded everyone's attention.

"Guys, I'm sorry that I have acted so selfishly for so long," he said. "None of you deserved how I treated you. I only thought about my own success. I have been an awful teammate, and I apologize for that. You've been like my family. In return, I have treated you like garbage. Starting now, I promise that I'll change."

His fellow Warriors beamed. They thanked him and started clapping slowly. Dashawn, who the team voted captain after the first game, spoke. "It's all good, man. It's in the past."

Ricky stuck his hand out, then Dashawn put his hand on top. The rest of the team followed suit.

"Warriors on three!" Ricky said. Finally, the star player acted like a leader.

Coach Daniels was taken aback. Seeing Ricky lead a team cheer was not what he expected after Ricky had abruptly left his office.

From that moment on, Ricky's negative and selfish attitude was gone. Ricky went to all of the practices and games. At times over the next few weeks, he acted as a waterboy, an assistant coach, and a cheerleader. He did not mind. If it helped the team, he did it.

The Warriors went on a winning streak. In the regular season, they beat the Durham Blue Devils, Charlesburg Cardinals, Greenbriar Bears, and Maple Valley Hawks. A few weeks later, the Warriors won a rematch against the Bears to become the Western Division champions.

10

For the first time in over ten years, Wellsport made it to the league championship game. As the winner of the Western Division, the Warriors had to play the Brockville Vikings, the Eastern Division winner. Both teams were undefeated entering the championship game.

History was on Brockville's side. The Vikings were used to winning championships. Over the last ten years, the Vikings had won seven league titles, five sectional championships, and three state titles.

The bus ride to Brockville was quiet. The only sounds Ricky heard were the rattling of the bus door and the shaking legs of nervous players.

The team had a lot on their minds. It felt as though the weight of the school was on their shoulder pads.

As Wellsport's winning streak gained momentum, more students and more town residents became interested in the team. Following the team's bus to Brockville were six more buses. There was one bus for cheerleaders and five more of students and fans making the ninety-minute trip.

The players arrived at the field and slowly shuffled off the bus. Ricky waited for his teammates to go first. As they walked closer to the field, they were amazed by the size of the stadium. It was a lot bigger than the Warriors' tiny home field.

As rock music blared from the stadium's speakers, the Warriors covered the ear holes of their helmets. It was the loudest they had ever heard a stadium, and the game hadn't even started yet.

Dashawn gathered the team and shouted over the music. "Okay, let's get in a line and walk to the field as a team."

The players lined up behind the bleachers of Brockville's massive stadium. They started to jog toward the field, but they stopped suddenly.

"Wow. We have to play . . . them?" the players said, pointing at their opponents. The Vikings greatly outnumbered the Warriors. Plus, these Vikings were giants.

"Yo, are these college kids?" Jerome said.

Size was not the only challenge the Warriors faced that day.

They continued their jog to the field. They stepped on the field, but they did not feel grass beneath their cleats. The field looked like grass, but it felt rubbery.

The Warriors were not used to playing on a field like that. They had only played on grass. Their school could not afford a state-of-the art field.

As Wellsport took to the field to warm up, the players were overwhelmed by the blinding stadium lights and the fans already in the stands.

Ricky glanced at Coach Daniels. He looked as overwhelmed as his players did. As Coach Daniels stared into the stands, Ricky noticed that his teammates were slipping anytime they made a cut in the opposite direction. It seemed like the Warriors were in for a long day on an unfamiliar field against a bigger, more experienced team.

11

Warm ups were over. Kickoff neared. The teams lined up behind the goalposts at opposite ends of the field. A few players were so energized they jumped up and down. "Let's do this!" they shouted.

The announcer's voice boomed over the buzzing crowd. The rich voice said, "And now, please welcome the visiting Wellsport Warriors." Ricky stood on the sideline and watched as his teammates rushed onto the field. The

Warriors' fans cheered so loudly that Ricky thought people in Wellsport could probably hear their roar.

For a brief moment, Ricky felt a tinge of jealousy. "No, they deserve this," he told himself. As his team took to the field without him, he clapped like thunder and howled like the winds of a tornado.

The voice returned. "Ladies and gentleman, please welcome the defending state champions, the Brockville Vikings!"

The roar from Brockville's hometown fans was even louder than Wellsport's.

The team captains met at midfield for the coin toss. Brockville's captain and star quarterback, Josh Winfield, called "heads." They won the toss and chose to receive the opening kickoff. Before heading to the sideline, Josh whispered to Wellsport's captains, "How'd you even make it this far? Get ready for a long game, losers." Josh sprinted away, but his arrogant laugh lingered.

For years, Ricky's teammates heard him boasting about himself to other teams but never anything *that* disrespectful. Since the first game of the season, when Ricky got penalized for taunting, Coach Daniels preached to his team to be good sports.

The moment finally arrived. It was time for kickoff. Brockville's returner Jake Hamilton, also Josh's main target in the passing game, awaited the kickoff. Eric ran toward the ball. He planted his foot to kick, but he slipped. As he was falling, his foot nudged the football. Brockville quickly jumped on the ball around midfield.

The Vikings cheered, as the Warriors went to their fallen teammate. Luckily, Eric was not injured. Still, the slip up gave the Vikings outstanding field position.

Josh's arrogant laugh returned. "Ha ha. I knew it was going to be easy, but this is too easy," he said.

The Vikings rushed to the line of scrimmage. Josh said, "Hut, hut." The ball was snapped. Brockville's offensive line shoved the Wellsport defenders to the ground. Josh took five steps back. He rolled to his right. He had all day to throw, but he did not need it. He saw Jake sprinting down the sideline. The cornerback, Vance Clark, had him covered. Josh pointed, then Jake made a quick cut inside. Jake faked out Vance. Vance slipped and landed flat on his back. Meanwhile, Jake kept running. Josh unleashed a deep bomb. Jake ran under it and strolled into the endzone. The extra point gave Brockville a 7-0 lead.

As Vance ran off the field, Josh said, "One play. One score."

Wellsport's first possession did not turn out much better. On the first play, Brockville's mountainous defensive end, Greg Dawson, overpowered Wellsport's offensive line. He smashed into Dashawn and stripped the ball. A linebacker scooped up the fumble and scored a touchdown.

The Vikings dominated the rest of the first half. Their size, strength, and quickness was too much for the Warriors. At halftime, Brockville led 28-0.

The Warriors headed to the north end of the field for halftime. Because of his crutches, Ricky lagged behind.

Josh ran up to Ricky. He smacked him on the shoulder. "Hey, nice crutches," he said. "I hear you're their best player. Now you're riding the pine." He gestured with his head toward the bench. "I've got news for you: It wouldn't matter if you played or not. We still would've crushed your sorry team."

Ricky remained silent.

Josh smirked, then chuckled. "You've got no heart. Just like your team," he said, before running after his teammates.

12

When Ricky finally made it to his team, he saw players hanging their heads. He saw his coach at a loss for words. The whole team was deflated. Their confidence was shot.

"Coach, can I say something?" Ricky asked.

"Go ahead, Ricky. I don't even know what to say right now," Coach Daniels said.

"Thanks." He gave his coach a polite nod. "Guys, we all know I was a jerk for the longest time. I only cared about myself. That was then. Now, I care about each of you. I care about this team."

A sad voice from the crowd said, "So?"

"So, before I turned my attitude around, I wanted to quit. I talked to coach. He told me that I couldn't go through life giving up when it was hard. He was right. That same lesson applies now."

"How?" said the same voice, sounding slightly less sad.

"Yeah, they've crushed us so far, but we owe it to ourselves, our school, and our town to keep fighting. The Vikings think we have no heart. I know we do. We have one half to prove them wrong. The final score won't really matter. What people will remember is if we gave up or not."

Voices from the crowd shouted different excuses.

"But they keep talking junk."

"We keep slipping."

"Their defensive end is too tough."

Ricky said, "I've got some ideas for all of those things. Why don't we turn those weaknesses into strengths?"

The team circled around Ricky. He borrowed Coach Daniels' dry-erase board. He diagramed a play to start the second half. The drawing highlighted each player's role.

Because the Vikings got the ball to start the game, the Warriors received the second-half kickoff. Marcus, Wellsport's best receiver, returned the kickoff to the thirty-five-yard line.

It was time to use one of Ricky's plays. Dashawn got under center. He said, "Ready. Set," then the ball was snapped. Greg powered over Wellsport's offensive line again. Keith, in at running back, blocked Greg. Greg muscled Keith to the ground. The giant defensive end closed in on Dashawn, who was scrambling in the backfield. Suddenly, Keith sprung to his feet. Dashawn zipped a pass over Greg's hands to Keith, who scampered sixty-five yards for the touchdown.

After the first touchdown, the defense gained more confidence and shut down Brockville's offense. They double-teamed Jake. They punished Josh anytime he had the ball.

"What's gotten into you?" Josh asked a group of Wellsport players.

"Pride," they said.

Brockville's once powerful defense could no longer stop Wellsport's clever offense. If a player slipped and fell to the ground, the Vikings did not know if it was for real or not. Plus, quick screen passes eliminated Brockville's greatest strength: Greg the Giant.

With no time remaining on the clock, Dashawn connected with Marcus for a long touchdown, making it 28-27. An extra point would send the game into overtime.

The crowd was deafening. Both sides screamed for their team. Wellsport's fans cheered for Eric to make the kick and send the game into overtime. Brockville's fans cheered for Eric to miss.

Eric nodded to Dashawn, who was the holder. The center snapped the ball to Dashawn. Eric glided toward the ball, but his plant leg slipped again. He landed on his back. The Warrior fans gasped. They thought they had lost. Dashawn scooped the ball up and ran to his right.

Jerome faked blocking, but he slipped past the line. He was wide open in the endzone. Dashawn lobbed a pass to Jerome.

"The two-point try is good!" the announcer said.

That was the plan all along. The coaches had decided to surprise the Vikings by going for the win. They instructed Eric to fall down like he did at the beginning of the game. They told everyone except for Dashawn and Jerome to act surprised when Eric fell.

The bus ride to Wellsport was much louder than the ride to Brockville earlier in the day. They had reason to be loud. The Warriors rallied to defeat the defending champions, 29-28. Players beamed as they took turns holding the league championship trophy.

13

The Warriors lost in the sectional title game, but they were not disappointed in the season they had. After all, they had won their first league title in over ten years.

At the awards banquet, Ricky won the most valuable player award.

"Even though Ricky only played part of the first game, this team could not have won without him. As the season went on, Ricky transformed. We all did. We all became champions," the coach said.

After the football season, Ricky still worked with Mr. Trout every day. Ricky's new attitude toward school and his hard work earned him a spot on the honor roll for each marking period.

The season Ricky spent riding the pine was the best one yet. The view from the sidelines gave Ricky a whole new view on life. From that angle, Ricky's future looked promising.

About The Author

Kyle A. Johnson is a former journalist turned urban educator in Rochester, New York. In his free time, Kyle works on a multitude of personal writing projects and freelances for local media outlets. Kyle contributed to the Story Shares contest because it combined two of his passions: writing and education. He firmly believes in the contest's mission to expose struggling readers to interesting and accessible books.

About The Publisher

Story Shares is a nonprofit focused on supporting the millions of teens and adults who struggle with reading by creating a new shelf in the library specifically for them. The ever-growing collection features content that is compelling and culturally relevant for teens and adults, yet still readable at a range of lower reading levels.

Story Shares generates content by engaging deeply with writers, bringing together a community to create this new kind of book. With more intriguing and approachable stories to choose from, the teens and adults who have fallen behind are improving their skills and beginning to discover the joy of reading. For more information, visit storyshares.org.

Easy to Read. Hard to Put Down.